AN ARK IN THE DARK

© 2018 by Creator's Toy Chest LLC

Published by Baker Books
A division of Baker Publishing Group
PO Box 6287, Grand Rapids, MI 49516-6287
www.bakerbooks.com

First Edition

Printed in the United States of America

Library of Congress Cataloging-in-Publication Data
Names: Blair, Brett, author. | Koenig, James, illustrator.
Title: An ark in the dark : Noah's story / Brett Blair ; illustrated by James Koenig.
Description: First edition. | Grand Rapids, MI : Baker Books, [2018] | Series: Creator's toy chest | Summary: Retells in verse the story of Noah's ark which saves two of every kind of animal while a flood purges the earth.
Identifiers: LCCN 2017040019 | ISBN 9780801017193 (cloth : alk. paper)
Subjects: LCSH: Noah (Biblical figure)—Juvenile fiction. | CYAC: Stories in rhyme. | Noah (Biblical figure)—Fiction. | Noah's ark—Fiction. | Animals—Fiction. | Deluge—Fiction. | Christian life—Fiction.
Classification: LCC PZ8.3.B575 Ar 2018 | DDC [E]—dc20
LC record available at https://lccn.loc.gov/2017040019

Published in association with the literary agency D.C. Jacobson & Associates, an Author Management Company, www.dcjacobson.com.

18 19 20 21 22 23 24   7 6 5 4 3 2 1

THE CREATOR'S TOY CHEST

AN ARK IN THE DARK

• Noah's Story •

Brett Blair

Illustrated by James Koenig

BakerBooks

a division of Baker Publishing Group
Grand Rapids, Michigan

• • •

To Nathan
The Strong

• • •

I am Noah.

I am building a boat.

God told me to build it.
He said it would float.

NO, NO, Noah!
You cannot make
A boat that big.
Oh, for goodness' sake.
It is too big.
It is too tall.
Boats aren't big.
Boats are small.

Yes! Yes, I say.
Oh, yes, I can.
I listen to God
And not to man.

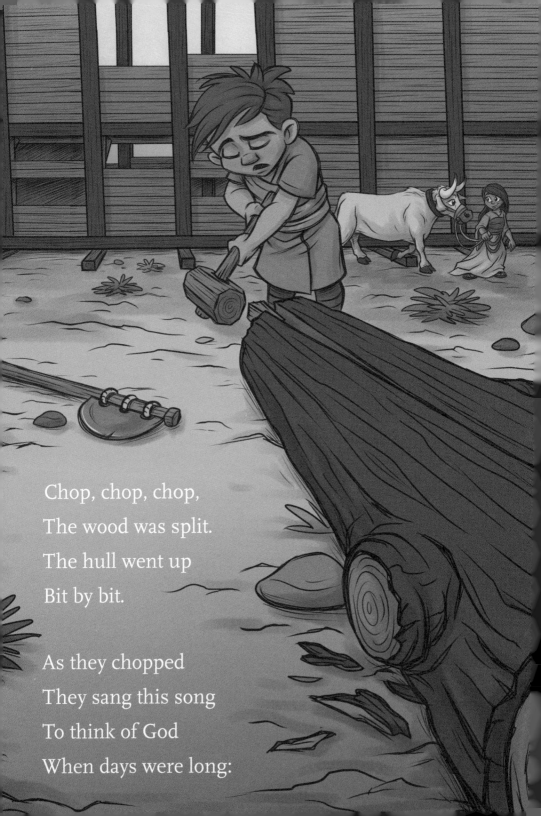

Chop, chop, chop,
The wood was split.
The hull went up
Bit by bit.

As they chopped
They sang this song
To think of God
When days were long:

"An ark in the dark
Will sail the seas
To save us all.
Oh, can't you see?

God's not happy
With what we've done.
We've wandered far
From where we've begun."

No. No, Noah!
You make a mistake.
God is unhappy?
Oh, give us a break.

It is too big.
It is too tall.
This story you tell
Makes no sense at all.

Yes. Yes, I say.
I say it is true!
God told it to me,
Now I'm telling you.

The rain will come.
I warn you all.
When it does,
It will fall

fall

fall.

God told Noah,
"Now it is time
To fill the ark
With all living kind.

Gather the creatures
That breathe and birth.
Save all life
Upon the earth."

"Two by two the bird and dog,
Save the fly and save the frog.

Two by two the wasp and bee,
Save the tick and save the flea.

Two by two the pig and bear,
Save the owl and save the hare.

Two by two the elk and moose,
Save the duck and save the goose."

But two by two, the people laughed.
"How will he save the two giraffes?"

"Go! Go, Noah,
Into the ark.
It's starting to rain.
The skies grow dark."

The heavens opened.
Rain came down.
Water covered
Every town.
Down it dripped,
Down it dropped.
Day and night,
It never stopped.

It filled creeks,
It filled streams,
And Noah heard
The people scream:

"Noah? Oh, Noah?
So, you were right.
It's getting deep,
And we thought you might
Open the ark.
Open the door,
And we won't laugh
Anymore."

But Noah yelled
At all these guys
A chilling message
In reply:
"The ark is full
From stem to stern.
You were warned,
But you didn't learn."

"Whoa, whoa, Noah!
These giant waves
Will send us all
To early graves."

"Have faith in God,"
Noah told his sons.
"God will finish
What he's begun.
This ark in the dark
Will sail the seas
To save us all.
Oh, can't you see?

God's not happy
With what we've done.
We've wandered far
From where we've begun.

But his hand is here
Within these walls.
He'll keep us dry
As this hard rain
falls
falls
falls."

And rain it did,
For weeks and weeks,
And covered all
The mountain peaks.

After months of rain,
As God had said,
All life on earth was gone
And dead.

On the mountain
Known as Ararat
The ark rested,
And there it sat.

Then one day,
At the break of dawn,
The sun came out.
The clouds were gone.

The winds blew.
The water went down.
Noah wondered,
Is there ground?

He thought about
God's promise and love,
And from a window
Flew out a dove.

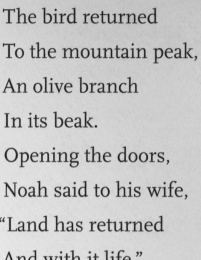

The bird returned
To the mountain peak,
An olive branch
In its beak.
Opening the doors,
Noah said to his wife,
"Land has returned
And with it life."

The crew all cheered,
And in Noah's heart,
Joy, relief,
A brand-new start.

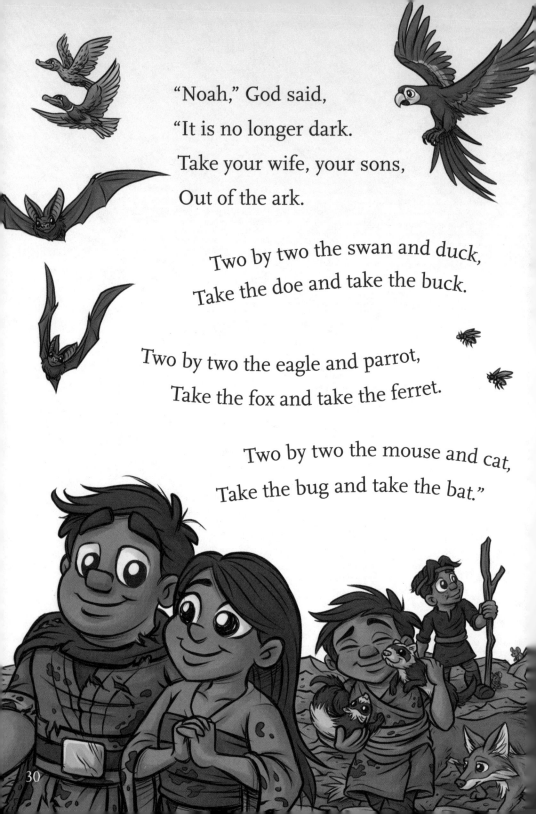

"Noah," God said,
"It is no longer dark.
Take your wife, your sons,
Out of the ark.

Two by two the swan and duck,
Take the doe and take the buck.

Two by two the eagle and parrot,
Take the fox and take the ferret.

Two by two the mouse and cat,
Take the bug and take the bat."

"Two by two the goat and ram,
Take the lion and take the lamb."

The last two made them laugh.
Bowed low the two giraffes.

31

God blessed Noah
And his sons.
"I know it is harsh
What I have done.

But what I did,
I did because of hate.
Men were mean,
Their sins were great.

But you were different.
You were grateful.
A heart of gold
And always faithful.

You did the right.
You did the good.
You did what I liked
The way you should."

After the rain
God drew a bow.
A promise of colors
So we all would know

That God forgives
All the day long,
When we are bad,
When we are wrong.

34

Red and orange
Yellow and green
Blue and violet
Indigo between.
Seven colors
To arc the sky
To tell us all
The reason why

35

An ark in the dark
Sailed the seas
To save us all
And set us free.